P9-DGR-507

One little wish.

Now what Kate didn't know about the Eddie Bestelli mitt was that it was indeed a magic mitt, and if you put your face close to it and made a wish, it would come true. So you can imagine how very surprised she was when she said to herself, with her eyes half-closed, "I would really like to try being a princess some-time," and then opened them up again to find herself sitting in a very uncomfortable chair and staring at a gray stone wall, with her mitt and a bowl of some weird dry stuff in her lap.

"Geez Louise!" said Kate. "What hap-pened?"

To Kate Krovatin and Caitlin Quindlen,
from Aunt Anna with love

PUFFIN BOOKS
Published by the Penguin Group
Penguin Putnam Inc., 375 Hudson Street, New York, New York 10014, U.S.A.
Penguin Books Ltd, 27 Wrights Lane, London W8 5TZ, England
Penguin Books Australia Ltd, Ringwood, Victoria, Australia
Penguin Books Canada Ltd, 10 Alcorn Avenue, Toronto, Ontario, Canada M4V 3B2
Penguin Books (N.Z.) Ltd, 182-190 Wairau Road, Auckland 10, New Zealand

Penguin Books Ltd, Registered Offices: Harmondsworth, Middlesex, England

First published in the United States of America by Viking,
a division of Penguin Books USA Inc., 1997
Published by Puffin Books,
a member of Penguin Putnam Books for Young Readers, 1999

14 16 18 20 19 17 15 13

Text copyright © Anna Quindlen, 1997
Illustrations copyright © James Stevenson, 1997
All rights reserved

THE LIBRARY OF CONGRESS HAS CATALOGED THE VIKING EDITION AS FOLLOWS:
Quindlen, Anna
Happily ever after / by Anna Quindlen ; illustrated by James Stevenson.
p.   cm.
Summary: When a girl who loves to read fairy tales is transported back to medieval
times, she finds that the life of a princess in a castle is less fun than she imagined.
ISBN: 0-670-86961-9
[1. Middle Ages—Fiction. 2. Princesses—Fiction. 3. Time travel—Fiction.]
I. Stevenson, James, ill. II. Title
PZ7.Q4192Hap 1997 [Fic]—dc20 96-36084 CIP AC

Puffin Books ISBN 0-14-038706-4

Printed in the United States of America
Set in Berling

Except in the United States of America, this book is sold subject to the condition
that it shall not, by way of trade or otherwise, be lent, re-sold, hired out, or otherwise circulated without the publisher's prior consent in any form of binding or
cover other than that in which it is published and without a similar condition
including this condition being imposed on the subsequent purchaser.

RL: 3.8

OTHER CHAPTER BOOKS FROM PUFFIN

Happily Ever After

by Anna Quindlen
illustrated by James Stevenson

PUFFIN BOOKS

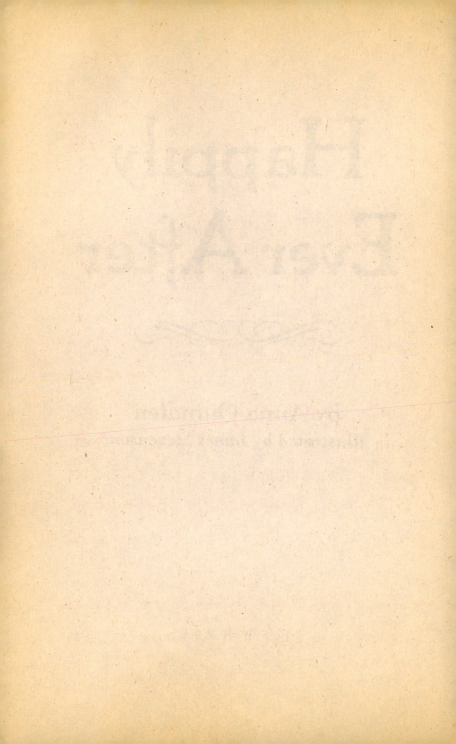

Chapter 1

Once upon a time, there was a girl named Kate. When her mother was cross with her, she called her Katherine, which was her real full name, and when her father was sweet with her, he called her Katydid, which was the name of a bug but Kate liked it anyhow.

Kate had long legs, with a scar running down the left one from the time she was wading in the creek where someone had thrown a piece of broken bottle. She had eyes the color of root beer and frizzy hair that was blondy-brown. She was the star shortstop on the Walker's Delicatessen Little League team, although she couldn't hit as well as she could field.

The funny thing about Kate was that while she was a girl who loved to hang upside down on the monkey bars, who could run faster than anyone in her class, and who never wore a skirt if she could help it, that's not all she was. The thing you'd never expect about her was that she also loved fairy tales. When she'd had a bad day at school, had a fight with her best friend Sarah, or brought up a big bruise on her knee falling while doing a cartwheel, she would run home, take the stairs

two at a time to her room, climb underneath her chubby comforter, and open the big book of fairy tales her aunt Mary had given her for her fifth birthday. She would read about frogs that were really princes, about battles between wizards and kings, about evil gnomes who tried to steal babies, and about beautiful princesses locked in towers.

Her aunt Mary had given Kate her baseball glove, too, an official Eddie Bestelli mitt. Eddie Bestelli was the batter who hit the home run that won the World Series for the New York Yankees in 1954, and the mitt had his signature on the side. Aunt Mary had gotten the mitt from her father for her birthday one year, and when she passed it on to Kate she took her out to the field where the Deli Demons played and sat her down on the home team's bench. "This is a very special baseball mitt," her aunt Mary said, looking Kate right in the eye. "Very, very special. I can't say more." Kate had thought that Aunt Mary was acting a little strange, but she did think the mitt had a nice deep pocket, and it improved her fielding a lot. Kate oiled it once a month.

One day Kate was reading, with her mitt beneath her pillow. She was reading a story about a princess with beautiful waving yellow hair, trapped in a tower by a dragon the color of pea soup. "Or boogers," thought Kate. Kate was not the kind of girl who thought about being pretty very much, but the princess looked so perfect in the pictures, with the little red jewels in her crown winking up from the page, that Kate said aloud to herself, "I would really like to try being a princess sometime."

Chapter 2

Now what Kate didn't know about the Eddie Bestelli mitt was that it was indeed a magic mitt, and if you put your face close to it and made a wish, it would come true. So you can imagine how very surprised she was when she said to herself, with her eyes half-closed, "I would really like to try being a princess sometime," and then opened them up again to find herself sitting in a very uncomfortable chair and staring at a gray stone wall, with her mitt and a bowl of some weird dry stuff in her lap.

"Geez Louise!" said Kate. "What happened?"

For a moment she was too surprised to move, and she just looked around the little circular room in which she sat. There was a pile of straw at one end, and a little round copper bowl with a handle at the other, and a few other chairs that looked as though they'd fall right down—*kerplunk!*—if you sat on them. Finally she looked down at herself. She was wearing a pink dress that laced up the front like a sneaker.

Kate poked her feet out in front of her and saw that she was wearing little leather slippers. Her hair was still the same color, that nice

warm shade of butterscotch-sundae topping, but it waved down her back and fell in little curlicues to her waist. Kate hiked up one side of her skirt and looked at her leg. Where the scar had once snaked up it, there was now only a smooth expanse of skin. It was no longer tanned and freckled, as Kate's legs always were from May to October. Her leg was as white as the looseleaf paper before you've started your homework.

"Holy moly," said Kate.

Suddenly Kate heard a loud noise from outside, as though someone had dropped a whole tray of silverware. She stood up, and something fell from her head to the stone floor with a clatter.

A gold circle lay at her feet, with the string of rubies on it winking up in the light that came through the slit windows in the stone walls. Kate looked down at the gold, the jewels, her clothes. She looked around.

"I'm a princess," she said softly to herself.

"Be gone, varlets!" she heard someone shout.

Kate leaped over her crown and ran to one of the tiny windows. In front of her were green fields, with here and there a blue ribbon of river. Vanishing along a dirt road were a dozen men on horseback. One was carrying a flag with blue and yellow stripes on a long metal pole. The horse's hooves were hidden in a thick cloud of gray-brown dust.

"Wait until I tell Sarah about this," said Kate. "She'll have a cow!"

"Ah, you wake," said a voice from below. "And just as I have vanquished your enemies."

Kate leaned a
little farther out
the tower window.
Below her was a
tall young man
wearing armor. His
hair was yellow and
curled around his hel-
met, which was pushed
back on his head. His
nose was straight, his
chin strong, his eyes
blue, his teeth white.
He looked as if some-
one had drawn him
with colored pencils
—which, Kate real-
ized when she

really thought about where she was, was probably exactly what had happened.

"Who were those guys?" said Kate.

"Ah, Princess," he said in a deep voice, "that is none of your affair. I will protect the tower. And after"—here his voice became deeper still—"we shall go to the king and seek his approval for our betrothal."

"I'm only in fourth grade," said Kate.

"Enough," said the prince—for Kate imagined that anyone with a voice that deep must either be a prince or a radio announcer. "Have you separated the wheat from the chaff?"

Kate looked behind her at the bowl she had found on her lap. The stuff inside looked a little like what Kate fed the hamsters in the science room at school. "I'm not sure," she said. When she looked back she could see a big cloud of dust coming down the road, and as she watched, the cloud became clearer and she could see the striped flag and the men on horseback galloping toward her.

"Big trouble," she yelled down to the prince, but he smiled and bowed and smiled and kissed his hand and waved and smiled and began to sing some song about picking roses and watching beauty fade. The sound of hooves kept getting louder and louder but the prince just kept on smiling and singing.

"*AAAAAaaaaahhhh!*" Kate yelled, and he finally stopped.

By the time the prince had knit his brow and kissed his hand one last time, the enemy was upon him. Kate had to admit it; his reaction time was bad, but he was a whiz with a sword. Soon most of the men had fallen off most of the horses and were scattered about on the green grass, groaning. Finally one, a man on a black horse with dark armor that seemed to swallow up all the sunlight, was fighting with the prince. Their swords clanged and clacked and clanged again, and Kate cheered when the prince moved forward and screamed

when he was forced back against the tower wall and yelled, "Get that guy!" and, "Go for it!" when the prince seemed to be making progress.

Chapter 3

But the prince did not make progress for long, and before Kate knew what was happening the knight on horseback—"probably the black knight," thought Kate, "but I don't think I'd read this part yet"—had pinned the prince against the tower and, with a sudden upward motion of his arm, flipped the prince's sword from his hand and onto the grass.

"Ah ha ha," cried the knight, with a sound

somewhere between a laugh and a shout.

"Jeepers creepers," yelled Kate. Looking around the tower for any kind of weapon, she saw only the copper pot on the far side of the stone floor. She hiked up her skirt, which was a real pain to run in, and raced over to grab it.

"Take that!" she yelled when she was back at the window, and she lobbed the pot at the knight and caught him square in the center of his forehead. For a moment his eyes widened, and then he fell forward onto the ground, out for the count.

"Cool," said Kate.

The prince went over and looked down at the knight, then up at Kate. He didn't seem as happy as Kate thought he ought to be. "Princess," he said, narrowing his eyes, "you

have vanquished your enemy. With a chamber pot."

"I couldn't let him kill you," Kate said.

"Ah," said the prince with a smile, and his white teeth sparkled in the sun. "Yes." He disappeared, and in a minute Kate heard him coming up the stairs to the tower. He bowed at the door, sat down on one of the chairs, and began to sing the roses song again.

After about a half hour of singing, punctuated by the occasional blown kiss, Kate had had it. "This is the most boring thing I've ever done in my life," she said to herself. She picked up the bowl that she'd found in her lap, but separating the wheat from the chaff didn't seem like a big improvement over staring at her hands, and she couldn't tell which part she was supposed to keep and which part she was supposed to throw away. From outside, she began to hear the sounds of people moving around, and once she heard what sounded like someone kicking the copper pot. Then there was the sound of horses galloping away from the tower. Through it all the prince smiled and sang. Kate began to do the multiplication tables in her head.

She'd gotten to eleven times nine and was starting to doze off when she began to smell a horrid smell. Then she heard a rumbling sound.

Kate went to the window. "Whoa!" she yelled. "Whoa, whoa, whoa!"

"Why so perturbed, Princess?" said the prince, who finally stopped singing.

"Whoa!" Kate said again. "Major reptile alert! Flames! Scales! Tiny little mean red eyes!"

"What sayest thou?"

"Geez Louise," said Kate. "It's a dragon, you dumbo!"

Chapter 4

And so it was. Kate thought the pictures didn't do him justice. For one thing, the flame came right out between his pointy teeth like a blowtorch. For another, he was a horrible slimy glittery green, like something in the fridge that had gone bad a long, long time ago.

And when a dragon was staring right at you and looking annoyed and famished at the same time, it was a completely different experience from seeing his picture in a book.

"Aha!" said the prince, and kissing his hand once more, he pulled his sword from its scabbard and rushed out of the room. Just then, the dragon ate the chamber pot, which had been left lying on the ground, and made a loud explosive noise, part burp, part roar.

Kate watched from the window as the prince slashed away at the dragon with his sword. But the big green guy had a neck as slippery and slithery as a snake, and he kept clear of the silver blade. No matter how the prince parried and thrust, he never got anywhere close to the dragon's chest and a blow to the heart. In fact, Kate noticed that the prince seemed to be doing nothing much but jabbing away at the air. She looked around for another copper pot, but she was out of pots and out of luck.

"Oh boy," said Kate. "We're in trouble here."

"I am blinded by the sun," the prince cried.

Kate could see that this was true. The dragon had the light behind him, but it was shining right in the prince's face. He couldn't see a thing.

"Hey!" Kate yelled. "Put your bill down."

"What?" the prince replied, still slicing at the air with his sword. The dragon swayed back and forth in the confident manner of a beast who knows dinner is only a heartbeat away, and dessert is waiting up in the tower. Tiny drops of saliva hung on the edge of his big wet dragon lips; they were a kind of sickly yellow color, and before they could fall to the ground, they sizzled and dried in the heat from his hot dragon breath.

"The thing on your helmet that goes in

front of your face. Push it up so it keeps the sun out of your eyes."

The prince did as Kate said, and the edge of his face mask, angled above his forehead, acted just like the bill of Kate's cap did on the ball-field. It cast a shadow over the top part of the prince's handsome face, and before the dragon knew what hit him, the prince's sword was buried up to its hilt in his snaky dragon neck. One last puff of orange smoke, and the dragon dropped into a pile, right on top of the prince.

All Kate could see of the prince were his black boots. At first she was afraid he was dead, but then his boots began to kick, and finally he got himself loose of the loops of dragon neck and rose to his feet, all green and glistening with slime. His blond hair was matted down, and he was making disgusting spitting noises.

Kate started to smile. Then she started to giggle. Finally she started to laugh out loud. The prince looked up, and he was most unhappy.

"Princess," he said darkly, wiping slime from his face, "now that I have slain the dragon"— here he put heavy emphasis on the word *I*— "we shall return to the royal castle." And he pulled his sword from the dragon's neck, wiped it on one leg, and disappeared around the side of the tower. In a moment, he was back on a big white horse. The horse was wearing a little velvet mask with gold stitching and a velvet blanket beneath his saddle. Kate came clatter-ing down the stairs. "If I get some scissors, I'm cutting a slit up the side of this skirt," she said to herself.

The prince lifted her into her saddle, then

vaulted up behind her. Kate had to sit sideways because of the stupid skirt. She held on tight to her Eddie Bestelli mitt. She didn't like the way the prince kept eyeing it, as though he thought he might like to have it himself. Plus, he was

singing again. And the dragon slime made him all sticky.

But the scenery was beautiful. The grass was greener than Kate had ever seen it, and some of the fields were dotted with tiny blue and yellow flowers, and others had fat brown cows cropping the grass. A small flock of blue-birds flew alongside them, chirping in time to the prince's song. Kate put out her hand, and one flew down and sat on her finger. A little breeze blew the curls around Kate's forehead, and the air smelled sweet and clean, the way it does just after the lawn's been mowed. Kate couldn't help it; she burst into song:

Have you ever gone fishing on a bright sunny day

And seen all the little fishies swimming all around the bay

With their hands in their pockets and their pockets in their pants,

And all the little fishies do the hoochie-coochie dance!

Chapter 5

Kate was just about to launch into the second verse when suddenly the bluebirds squawked, the horse reared, and a bolt of lightning flashed through the sky above them. They had gone around a curve in the road, and all at once they found themselves in thick forest, dim and dark, cold and creepy. Standing in the middle of the road was an old woman in a black cloak, with a long curving nose and wild white hair like a cloud around her head. A crow sat on her shoulder, and next to her was a little man carrying a sack.

"Right on time, Prince," said the old woman in a quavering, wavering voice. "Hand her over or I'll turn you into a wart hog."

Kate looked around the forest. There were a good number of wart hogs standing around under the trees. They had tusks that curled like commas and gray bristly hair. They looked back at Kate sadly. One was wearing a crown. There was a long silence. The bluebirds had fled. Kate clutched her mitt to the front of her pink dress.

"Princess, I fear I must bid you farewell," said the prince. He gave her a little nudge, and she slid down the side of the big white horse.

"You're just going to leave me here?" Kate

said, but before she could even finish the sentence, the prince had turned his horse and galloped away.

"What a wimp!" said the witch.

"But handsome," said the little man.

"Handsome is as handsome does," said the witch. "What's with the big leather glove?"

Kate realized the witch was talking to her, and she curtseyed slightly and said, "It's my baseball mitt, your badness."

"I like this girl," said the witch.

The witch and the troll tied Kate's hands behind her back, and the troll put her Eddie Bestelli mitt in his sack. The two flanked her as they marched through the forest. They had walked for several miles when it began to get even darker, not the dark of shadows but the dark of night. Bats began to whirl around them

like black leaves drifting through the tree branches, and the sound of an owl's flutey hooting came from the thickest part of the forest.

When there was no light at all, the witch untied Kate and put her to work gathering sticks, and soon they had a fire going in a clearing surrounded by enormous evergreens. The witch began to mutter mystical words, and as the troll and the witch faced one another, the fire made weird shadows on their faces, and the witch's eyes glowed red. The troll smiled and reached into his sack, and Kate got goose bumps all up and down her arms and legs. Then he pulled out some bits of silver, and something round and red, and laid them in front of the witch.

"Jacks!" Kate said.

"What?" said the witch.

"You're playing jacks." And Kate reached over and bounced the red rubber ball and picked up a jack, then two, then three. She messed up on foursies, because she was still nervous about everything that was happening.

"I really like this girl," said the witch. "Gimme a turn." At first she had a hard time palming the jacks, but Kate told her everyone did in the beginning, and by the time the fire was starting to falter, they'd all three had a good game.

"We took these off another princess a couple of years back, but we didn't know what to do with them," said the troll.

"Nor this," said the witch. She stuck her head into the bag and came out with a flashlight, and handed it with a grin to Kate.

"Oh," said Kate, "you need batteries for that.

But look." And Kate leaned forward with a stick in her hand and taught the witch and the troll to play tic-tac-toe in the dirt. She taught them to sing the fishies song and to do the hokey-pokey.

"You put your whole nose in," sang the witch in her gravelly voice, "you take your whole nose out . . ."

Then they stoked the fire some more and the troll put on a pot of water. Kate's heart rattled around in her chest like a hamster in an exercise wheel.

"Is it time to eat me?" she said.

"Eat you!" cried the witch. "After all the games you taught us? What kind of people do you think we are! Besides, we never eat princesses. Even the really boring ones who sit here all night shivering and crying, or the ones

who whine that we're keeping them away from their needlework. We wouldn't eat you. That's a myth. Anyway, you're the best princess we've ever had."

"Don't forget that one who taught us how to use a bow and arrow," said the troll.

"Well, all right," said the witch. "You're one of the best princesses we've ever had. We wouldn't eat you. Yucch. Imagine."

"Then what will you do with me?" Kate said.

The witch sighed. "I wish we could keep you," she said. "The truth is we only kidnap all of you because we're so lonely out here. Sometimes we get a flute from one of you, or a book, and it helps pass the time. Nobody's ever taught us as much as you have. Do know any more games?"

Kate thought for a moment. "I could teach you to play poker for peanuts." Then she shook her head. "We don't have any cards," she said.

"Or peanuts," said the troll.

"Well," sighed the witch, "you've done enough. Tomorrow you'll meet your fate, as the others have. I'm sorry."

Chapter 6

Kate scarcely slept at all that night. There was a big round white moon overhead that shone down when the clouds were blown aside, and the forest sounds and her fear of tomorrow made it hard for her to sleep. Just before dawn, two bears lumbered by, but they only whispered, "Sleep tight," and moved on.

At sun-up, the witch and the troll marched off with Kate again, but they left her hands free

and she taught them to sing the happy birthday song, the one where you look like a monkey and act like one too. The witch sang it so much that Kate wound up telling her some elephant jokes just to stop her singing, which sounded a little like rocks rolling around in a can.

Finally they came out of the forest to a meadow that seemed to stretch on forever. There was nothing but grass as far as Kate could see, except for a great gray castle on the horizon with red and gold flags flying from its four corners.

"There you go," said the troll. "There's the castle."

"That's what you're going to do with me? Bring me back?"

The witch frowned. "Now, you're not going

to be one of those ones who cries and carries on and wants to stay in the woods with us, are you? Because we can't do that or we'd get in trouble."

"No," said Kate. "But can I have my mitt back?"

"What's it do?" said the witch.

"Catches baseballs."

"Do we have any baseballs?"

Kate shook her head.

"Give it to her," the witch said. The troll tossed Kate her Eddie Bestelli mitt, and Kate tucked it under her arm and trudged toward the castle. The sun was full in her eyes, and she wished she had her Deli Demons cap. Behind her, she could hear two voices raised in song:

"Happy birthday to you. Happy birthday to you ..."

"My mom would say that this dress looks like I've slept in it," thought Kate. "But this time I really did sleep in it."

As Kate got nearer the castle there were muffled shouts and the blare of trumpets from the little towers atop each corner. Then the big arching front door opened and a group of knights on horseback galloped toward her. Kate couldn't wait to see the prince and tell him exactly what she thought about a person who pushed another person off his horse and then left her to the witches and the trolls. Although now that Kate had met the witch and the troll, she was glad she had. But still. No member of the Deli Demons would ever have left her stranded on base the way that stupid prince had ditched her in the forest.

But when the knights had stopped in front of her, removed their helmets, and bowed their shaggy heads, she could see that the prince was not with them.

"Princess," said one. "This is a happy day. You have been saved. First the kidnapping by the evil elves, then being sold to the black prince, and finally the dark witch of the forest."

"Wow," thought Kate. "I missed most of the worst stuff. I wonder what the evil elves were like."

"Who is it who has rescued you?" said the knight. "He will surely be well rewarded."

"I rescued myself," said Kate. "It wasn't much of a rescue, really. The witch and the troll were nice."

The knight bowed his head. "She is bewitched," he said sadly to the others.

Kate brought her fist into her mitt with a thump. "I most certainly am not," she said.

The knights tried to get her onto one of their horses, but Kate said she'd prefer to walk back. At the door she could see a group of girls in dresses like her own, in all different colors, like a bag of M&M's. They were waving and cheering. When she got inside, they curtseyed and surrounded her in a little circle. Before she knew it, she was upstairs in another room with gray stone walls, and two of the bigger girls were trying to get her into a tub of hot water. Kate made them all wait outside while she took a bath. None of them had a pair of scissors, but one had a little blade she used for cutting her sewing thread, and Kate used it to slit her dress up the side. When the girls saw this, they all slit their dresses, too.

For dinner they had roast wild boar, big
round pale things that looked like giant
turnips, and crusty loaves of brown bread. Kate
ate a lot of bread.

"To the princess!" shouted the big knight
who'd met her in the meadow, raising his cup,
and everyone shouted, "To the princess!" and

Kate gave them all a big thumbs-up.

"Cheers, big ears!" Kate cried back.

At first they looked puzzled, but then they tried it out, and by the end of the evening they were all giving each other the thumbs-up sign, even her ladies-in-waiting, and shouting, "Cheers, big ears," until Kate's own ears were aching.

Chapter 7

Next morning, when Kate woke up because a couple of the girls were sprinkling rosewater on her bed, all the knights had left to look for the king and the prince, who were off with some of the castle's fiercest warriors trying to rescue her from the witch.

"Rescue, my foot," Kate muttered.

"We will work on the king's jerkins today," said one of her ladies-in-waiting, whose name was Ann. And she began to divide up a great pile of leather hides. "There are eight of us," she added, "nine including you, my princess. Would you like to read aloud to us while we work?"

"I would like to have some fun," said Kate, and suddenly she looked around at the eight ladies and the pile of jerkin leather and began to grin.

"Change of plans!" she cried, handing her Eddie Bestelli mitt to Ann.

Well, you can imagine how surprised the rescue party was two days later when they rode back to the castle and found themselves in the middle of the ninth inning of a game between the Ladies-in-Waiting and the Serving Maids, with the Maids winning four to two. "Pray, sir, get out of the outfield," yelled Ann as one of the knights came galloping toward her, and he pulled his horse up short. Kate was pitching. The girls had taken to baseball a lot faster than she would have bet, particularly using those flimsy mitts they'd stitched together, but none of them could pitch overhand to save their lives. On the other hand, the serving maids could hit. Hard. One of them had found a

big paddle the cook used to make butter down in the castle dairies. When one of the maids connected with that thing, the ball they'd made out of strips of rags and leather flew almost back to the treeline where Kate had last seen the witch and the troll. She felt sad that the two of them couldn't be there to learn to hit and field.

The scullery maid was up at the plate, and she looked mean. This was mainly because she had little eyes and a big plump face and she squinted into the sun, but Kate was taking no chances. She threw a fast ball, and the maid fanned it.

"Strike one!" Kate called. She'd explained that it was pretty unusual for the pitcher to be the umpire, too. But no one else knew the game well enough.

"Princess!" came a voice like a clear deep horn.

"Can't talk now," she cried, and threw another fastball. The maid fanned it again.

"She is indeed bewitched," she heard behind her, and she called without turning around, "Am not, hamhead!" Her ladies-in-waiting all giggled. "Pay attention!" Kate yelled. And she threw the ball again, and this time the maid connected with a great big whack.

Kate watched as the ball soared over her head. As it flew, the leather cover came loose and dropped to the ground, and the ball of rags unraveled.

"That's the game, team," Kate called.

"We won?" said Ann.

"We lost five-two," Kate said, shaking hands with the scullery maid, who had stopped squinting and had a big smile on her moon face.

"But princesses never lose," said Ann.

"Princess, schmincess—in baseball, effort is what counts," said Kate. "That's what my coach says."

"Princess, schmincess," Ann repeated, nodding. "Cheers, big ears!" But just as Kate was smiling at her and giving her the thumbs-up sign, Ann's eyes got big and she dropped down into a low curtsey. Kate turned, and there on the biggest horse she'd ever seen was a man who seemed almost as big, sitting way up there with the late-day sun behind him. He had a thick white beard and a curling mane of white hair. His eyes were blue. As she stared at him, he slipped from the back of the big horse and looked Kate up and down. He stared at her mitt, then into her eyes, and he looked puzzled.

"Princess," he said, "your adventures have changed you greatly."

Then suddenly right behind him was the prince. Of course he didn't look at Kate, or she would have given him her I-don't-like-you-one-bit stare, which was pretty famous in her fourth-grade class, although she didn't use it much.

"As I said, your highness," said the prince, "I fear she has been bewitched."

Chapter 8

"Oh, oh, oh, oh, oh!" cried Kate, stamping her foot. "Will everyone stop this bewitched stuff! I'm fine. He's the one who ditched me in the forest without even putting up a fight when the witch showed up."

"Is this true?" asked the king.

"Sire, it seemed to me that the best way to secure the safety of the princess—"

"Oh, pooh," said Kate. "He just wanted

to save his own skin. Even the witch called him a wimp."

"Princess, what thing is this, this *wimp*?"

"Never mind," said Kate. "The point is, I bonked the black knight, I helped slay the dragon, and I went off with the witch and wound up back here, and he did nothing. Zip. Zilch."

"Zilch?" said the king, twisting his beard with his fingers.

"She is unhinged by her misadventures," said the prince. "Perhaps the royal physician should see her."

"I'm not unhinged," said Kate, and she sat down in the grass and put her mitt in her lap and her head in her hands. She could see it now: years of separating wheat and chaff, watching from windows, working on tapestries and jerkins, and listening to the prince sing. Kate didn't cry much. She hadn't even cried when they stitched up her leg in the emergency room. But she could feel the tears beginning to rise behind her eyes. She missed her best friend Sarah and her parents, her Little League coach Mr. Benson and her teacher Mrs. Howe, her dog Dawg, and even her little brother Nathaniel, who usually drove her completely nuts, saying "can I play?" whenever her friends were over and she didn't want him around.

"I want to go home," whispered Kate to herself—and to her Eddie Bestelli mitt, too. And the meadow, the maids, the prince, the king, everything vanished with the last breath of her last word, and Kate was in her own bed again, with Dawg licking her fingers with his big pink piece-of-ham tongue.

(Oh, and about the prince: the poor guy went a little crazy after the princess simply disappeared before his very eyes. Plus, everyone in the castle suspected that Kate had been telling the truth, and they all looked at him a little differently, and from time to time one of the small boys would whisper, "wimp," as he passed by. He wound up roaming the countryside ever after, singing and bowing to complete

strangers, who would shake their heads and give him a few pence, although after a while they got so sick of the whole thing that they would cross a field to avoid him when they saw him coming.

But the Ladies-in-Waiting played the Maids in baseball every week—Ann learned to pitch, with a whole lot of practice—and after a while they even taught the knights how to play, too.)

Kate was so happy to be at home that she hugged Dawg, and she ran her finger up and down the scar on her (very tanned) leg and she looked out the window at her street, which was a normal street on a normal late afternoon with the sun going down slowly behind Jennifer Fabrikant's house at the end of the block. She looked in the mirror at her own short frizzy hair, and she looked at the princess in the book, who had the same faint gentle smile she had always had. Except, Kate realized, that if you looked closely, her pink dress was slit up one side.

And then she went downstairs to get a banana, because she was starved. She kept thinking of what Aunt Mary sometimes said: "Be careful what you wish for; you might get it." Kate knew that was true, because she'd wanted to be a flower girl in her cousin Adrienne's wedding, and then she'd had to wear a dress with a net petticoat that scratched her legs like crazy. But now more than ever Kate understood that sometimes the things you think you want aren't really what you want at all.

Chapter 9

The next time Kate saw her aunt Mary, she took her out into the backyard and looked her right in the eye. "I need to ask you about my baseball mitt," Kate said.

Her aunt Mary grinned at Kate, and her eyes sparkled in the sunshine. For just a moment she looked like a girl herself, young, maybe younger than Kate. "Just keep it oiled," her aunt Mary said to Kate, "that's all."

But if you think Kate stopped liking fairy tales, you're wrong. She just had a lot more sympathy for the trolls and witches who were always casting spells over handsome young princes, and she had a healthy respect for dragons, and she understood that life in a tower was not all it was cracked up to be. And sometimes, when she'd had tough day, she'd crawl beneath her comforter and reread the stories she'd read so many times before.

And she read happily ever after. And the Deli Demons won the county championship, and Kate hit a grand slam in the winning game.

Anna Quindlen is a Pulitzer Prize-winning journalist and the author of fiction for both adults and children. Ms. Quindlen, her husband, and their three children live in Hoboken, New Jersey.

James Stevenson has written and/or illustrated more than eighty books and drawn more than seventy covers and countless cartoons for *The New Yorker* magazine. Mr. Stevenson lives with his family in Connecticut.